DC SUPER HERO
FAIRY TALES

LITTLE ROBIN'S
FIGHTING HOOD

D1407709

BY SARAH HINES STEPHENS
ILLUSTRATED BY AGNES GARBOWSKA
COLORS BY SIL BRYS

BATMAN CREATED BY
BOB KANE WITH BILL FINGER

STO

Published by Stone Arch Books, an imprint of Capstone
1710 Roe Crest Drive, North Mankato, Minnesota 56003
capstonepub.com

Library of Congress Cataloging-in-Publication Data
Names: Hines Stephens, Sarah, author. | Garbowska, Agnes, illustrator.
Title: Little Robin's fighting hood / by Sarah Hines Stephens ; illustrated
by Agnes Garbowska.
Description: North Mankato, Minnesota : Stone Arch Books, an imprint
of Capstone, [2021] | Series: DC super hero fairy tales | Audience:
Ages 8–11. | Audience: Grades 4–6. | Summary: Robin sets off to deliver
an important package to Batman, but on the way he runs into Catwoman,
and barely escapes; arriving at his destination, he finds that Batman
is a prisoner—and it is up to Robin to use his cape and hood to catch
Catwoman and free his mentor.
Identifiers: LCCN 2021015968 (print) | LCCN 2021015969 (ebook) |
ISBN 9781663910554 (hardcover) | ISBN 9781663921291 (paperback) |
ISBN 9781663910523 (pdf)
Subjects: LCSH: Robin, the Boy Wonder (Fictitious character)—Juvenile
fiction. | Batman (Fictitious character)—Juvenile fiction. | Catwoman
(Fictitious character)—Juvenile fiction. | Superheroes—Juvenile fiction.
| Supervillains—Juvenile fiction. | Fairy tales—Adaptations. | CYAC:
Fairy tales. | Superheroes—Fiction. | Supervillains—Fiction. | LCGFT:
Superhero fiction. | Fairy tales.
Classification: LCC PZ8.H544 Li 2021 (print) | LCC PZ8.H544 (ebook) |
DDC 813.6 [Fic]—dc23
LC record available at https://lccn.loc.gov/2021015968
LC ebook record available at https://lccn.loc.gov/2021015969

Designed by Hilary Wacholz

TABLE OF CONTENTS

ONCE UPON A TIME ...

THE WORLD'S GREATEST
SUPER HEROES COLLIDED WITH
THE WORLD'S BEST-KNOWN
FAIRY TALES TO CREATE ...

DC SUPER HERO
FAIRY TALES

Now, Robin is setting off to deliver parts for an alarm system to Batman on the other side of Gotham City. But on the way, he has a run-in with the big, bad Catwoman that puts the whole mission at risk in this twisted retelling of "Little Red Riding Hood"!

CHAPTER 1

ROBIN TO THE RESCUE

Like most children in Gotham City, young Tim Drake grew up idolizing the city's greatest hero—Batman! Tim papered his room with newspaper clippings of the Super Hero's good deeds. He dreamed of meeting the Dark Knight and maybe even working by his side one day.

As fate would have it, that day came before Tim was grown. Tim's father died, leaving him an orphan. He was soon adopted by the famous billionaire Bruce Wayne.

To others, it seemed like the boy had gotten a lucky break, being taken in by such a wealthy guardian. Tim knew he was even luckier than he appeared. Because Bruce Wayne was not just rich—he had a powerful secret.

Bruce was actually Batman. The boy had been adopted by his hero! Even better, the Dark Knight agreed to train Tim Drake to become his new sidekick, Robin the Boy Wonder.

Tim worked hard and learned quickly. Fighting for what was right felt like the job he was born to do! And as Robin, working alongside Batman, he got that chance.

One autumn day, Tim was interrupted at school with a new Super Hero mission.

BZZZ! BZZZ!

The watch that Batman had given him buzzed on his wrist. A message flashed on the tiny screen. It read: *REPORT TO THE BATCAVE IMMEDIATELY.*

Tim's eyes grew wide. His hand shot up in the air.

"I need to leave early. It's a family emergency," he told his teacher.

The teacher gave a nod, and Tim rushed from the room.

That wasn't even a lie, the boy thought as he ran down the hallway. *Batman asked me to come immediately. This could be a* real *emergency!*

Tim rushed out of school and caught the first bus he could. He tapped his feet impatiently as the bus wound its way to the edge of Gotham City.

When they were close to Wayne Manor, Tim jumped off and ran to the mansion.

The boy let himself in with a code and hurried down a secret passage to the lair that lurked below the main house. He arrived out of breath and looked around for Batman. Tim was ready to rush off on a rescue adventure!

But Batman was nowhere to be found. Only Alfred appeared from a secret doorway.

"There you are, Master Drake," said the tall, white-haired butler. He spoke and moved deliberately. He certainly didn't seem to be in a hurry.

"I left school as soon as I got the message!" Tim said breathlessly. "What's going on? Where is Batman? He said to come immediately!"

Alfred strolled over to a large workbench. Its surface was covered in fancy gadgets. But the butler stopped next to the two most ordinary-looking objects: a yellow cape and a silver case with a long strap.

"Ah, yes. Thank you for coming so quickly," the butler continued calmly, ignoring Tim's questions. "I have a very important task for you."

"Wait. *You* have a task?" Tim said. His shoulders dropped. It wasn't Batman who had called him in. It had been Alfred.

"Batman *and* I," Alfred said. "We have an important job that you must do alone."

Tim felt his pulse quicken. He drew in a breath. As the Boy Wonder, Robin usually worked *alongside* Batman.

But this was different. They wanted him to do a job on his own!

"What is it?" Tim asked.

He was already imagining what his mission would be. *Do they want me to sneak into The Joker's lair to dig up important info?* he wondered. *Tail the evil Penguin to a crime scene? Rescue innocent captives?*

"I need you to take this package to Batman," Alfred said, patting the silver case on the workbench.

Tim let out a puff of disappointment. Delivering a package did not sound at all like the exciting mission he had been hoping for!

Alfred noticed the boy's frown. "This is a very important task, I can assure you!" the butler said.

Tim stood up straighter. He didn't mean to be ungrateful. He was, of course, willing to help, but he wanted to solve crimes and fight for justice! Not . . . deliver packages.

"At this moment, Batman is working to set up a state-of-the-art alarm system at the Gotham City Art Museum," Alfred explained. "As you may have heard, the House of Jelenia's jewelry exhibit is coming to town. The Dewdrop Diamond—the largest green diamond in the world—is to be shown publicly there for the first time!"

"I think I saw something about that on the news," Tim replied, trying not to sound glum. "The exhibit will open next month, right?"

"Correct," Alfred said. "But what you haven't heard is that the jewels arrived *early*."

"Early?" Tim repeated. "So that means . . ."

"The alarm system wasn't in place yet," Alfred finished. "That is why the museum contacted Batman. They have asked him to complete the job there, so he can protect the jewels as he works. He cannot leave until the alarm is up and running. He cannot even retrieve these final parts that have just arrived. So, he has asked you to deliver them. Personally."

"What's so important about the parts that Batman needs *me* to bring them?" Tim asked.

"Inside this case are thirteen crystals that will be used in the oscillating alarm system," Alfred explained. "They are a key component. The crystals vibrate at a high frequency. Once installed, any movements interrupting their delicate vibrations will trigger the alarm."

The butler opened the case and lifted out a crystal. It glittered even in the dim light.

"The crystals themselves are worth quite a bit of money, although not nearly as much as what they will protect!" Alfred continued. "And this delivery must be made tonight in absolute secret, so that no one discovers the Dewdrop Diamond is unprotected. Are you up for the task?"

"You bet!" Tim replied. He was starting to feel better about the whole thing. Speed and secrecy definitely added a touch of excitement to the job. He held out his hands for the container.

"Not so fast," Alfred said. He placed the crystal back in the case and kept it just out of the boy's reach. He held out the folded yellow cape that was on the bench instead. "I want you to wear this."

Tim was confused. As Robin, he always wore a yellow cape along with his red shirt and mask.

"But I already have a—" he started to say.

FWOOOSH!

Alfred shook out the garment. Tim could now see that it was larger and longer than the cape he usually wore. It also had a black hood. The butler handed it to the boy.

"Keep the hood up to hide your identity," the butler said. "If anyone should spot Batman's sidekick carrying a locked case, they might get suspicious."

Robin nodded, but Alfred was not finished.

"Never let the container out of your hands," he went on. "And follow the path I have laid out."

Alfred pushed some buttons on a nearby computer. A map popped up on Tim's wrist screen. A red dotted line made a trail across Gotham City. It avoided all the busier areas.

"Whatever you do, do not stray from this path, or stop to talk to anyone on your way," Alfred said. He caught Tim's eyes and stared at him sternly. "Is that clear?"

The butler was not as intimidating as Batman, but Tim respected him. He nodded and said, "Understood."

Tim tapped the wrist screen to hide the map. Then he stepped into a small room off the larger chamber to change. He re-emerged as Robin the Boy Wonder!

Robin swung the new cape over his shoulders. He pulled up the hood. It cast his face in shadow.

Alfred nodded in approval—the boy's identity was hidden. At last, the butler handed Robin the container of crystals.

"Stay safe, young Robin," Alfred said. "And remember my words. Go straight to the museum. Do not stop along the way. Do not let that case out of your sight. And do not talk to strangers!"

CHAPTER 2

ALONG THE PATH

With his face hidden and the container filled with crystals strapped across his chest, Robin set off. He followed the route to the museum that Alfred had chosen for him.

It was definitely not the fastest route through Gotham City, but it was the most discreet. Alfred's path avoided the crowded, popular areas of downtown. Instead, it took Robin along the edge of the city, close to the docks.

The streets by the water were mostly empty. The only things moving were a few alley cats out looking for scraps. Dark, heavy rain clouds overhead blocked the late afternoon sun. They made everything look gloomy.

Robin kicked a stray can. It clattered down the street and banged against a wall.

CLANK!

Robin sighed. The excitement of his secret mission had quickly worn off. Delivering a package—even if it did hold something important and valuable—was boring. Robin caught up to the can and kicked it again.

CLANK!

He listened to the clanging echo on the empty street. It faded to silence. Then Robin heard something else . . .

CRREEEEEAAK!

It sounded like a crooked window being forced open. An anxious whisper followed soon after.

Robin crouched low and peered around the corner. The dark, narrow alley was filled with garbage. A rat skittered by. Other than that, all was still.

Robin was still too. He watched the alley for several long moments, looking up and down. He felt certain the sounds had come from this direction.

Robin glanced at his watch. He wanted to investigate. Alfred had told him to stay on the path. But Batman was always telling him to trust his gut. Right now, Robin's gut was saying loudly that something was up. Something sinister.

Finally, Robin heard another noise.

PSSSST!

The sound was coming from an open window overhead. Robin darted to the other side of the alley and flattened himself against the wall. From there, he could see a man standing in a dark window frame.

The man was wearing a mask. It seemed as if he was trying to signal to someone. He looked nervous.

"Hey," the man called in a loud whisper. There was no answer.

FWHEEEET!

He whistled through his teeth. The sound echoed against the brick buildings. At last, a second figure came out from behind a dumpster.

She was also masked and dressed in dark colors. After looking around in both directions, she waved to the man in the window.

Robin held his breath. The whispering. The masks. The sneaking around. His gut was right. These people were definitely up to no good! Forgetting all about his promise to Alfred to stay on the path, he moved farther into the alley to get a better look.

"Toss it here!" the woman on the ground called in a harsh whisper.

"Quiet! You trying to get us in trouble?" the man at the window hissed back, making even more noise than his partner.

The man disappeared from view. When he came back, he was holding something in his hands.

"I am trying to keep us *out* of trouble," the woman spat back. "We were supposed to be done with this job an hour ago!"

Robin smiled to himself. These thieves didn't seem very smart. They also had no idea he was watching them. They would be easy to wrap up!

"Now just throw it down so we can get out of here!" the woman said. She held out her arms.

The man in the window tossed a large package to the waiting woman. She caught it with a grunt and staggered back.

A split second later, a rope appeared out the window. The man came next. He slowly crawled down the rope so the pair of criminals could make their escape.

Or so they thought! Robin prepared to pounce.

But as he moved, the hard case slung around his shoulder fell forward. It bumped awkwardly against his chest.

The young hero grabbed the strap and hesitated. He had promised Alfred that he wouldn't stray from the path or leave the package for any reason.

But Alfred didn't know that I would stumble on a crime in progress, he thought.

Pushing away his doubts, Robin lifted the strap over his head. He tucked the container behind a sack of trash.

Stopping these thieves won't take long, he thought. *The crystals will be safe, and I'll be back on my way in no time!*

Feeling sure of his decision, Robin stepped into the center of the alley. He knocked back his hood, so his vision would be clear and he would be ready for action. He stood tall and placed his hands on his hips.

The Boy Wonder didn't care if the thieves saw him now. He hoped his strong stance would strike the same fear into their hearts that Batman's appearance might. He held his right hand up, with the palm outstretched.

"Halt!"

The loud command echoed down the alley. But Robin had not spoken a word!

CHAPTER 3

Cat Burglars

The two criminals stopped in their tracks, and Robin whirled around to see who had shouted. He thought he was the hero about to stop a crime in progress! Instead *he* had been stopped in his tracks. But by who?

When he saw the slim figure crouched on top of the dumpster, Robin balled up his fists. The shadowy form moved with feline grace. A woman dressed in black with pointed ears slipped out of the dark.

"Catwoman!" Robin said.

"Well hello, Robin," the cat burglar replied. A smile spread across her face. "I didn't recognize you before, in that hood. But I should have known that it would be Batman's little bird meddling in my business."

"And I should have known you were behind this burglary!" Robin shouted back. He and Batman had faced off with the skilled Super-Villain thief many times before. "So those are your goons." He tipped his head back toward the masked man and woman.

Behind him, Robin could hear the thieves creeping closer. He was caught between the three crooks. Trapped.

Catwoman's laugh was like a purr. "You look nervous, Boy Wonder."

She leaped from the dumpster and landed silently in front of Robin. The criminal was now blocking his exit out of the alley.

Catwoman took a step forward. Robin took a step back.

He quickly glanced over his shoulder. The important case of crystals was still hidden behind the trash bag. He needed to get to it before someone else did!

"What are you doing, out by yourself?" Catwoman asked. She craned her long neck. "And what's that you're trying to hide?"

Without looking away from Catwoman, Robin crouched down. Then he spun and made a blind dive for the case. But he came up short. All he was able to grab was a fistful of garbage.

"Rats!" he hissed.

The Boy Wonder couldn't pause. He sprang up and flipped in midair. He landed on the other side of the two goons who were rushing in to grab him!

Without giving the man or woman time to think, Robin delivered a high kick.

BAM!

He sent the man sprawling.

The woman was quicker. She came back with a powerful kick of her own.

Robin caught her foot midair. He yanked it, trying to topple the woman. But she kept her balance and pulled closer to Robin. Then, she drove her head into the boy's.

CRACK!

Lights flashed in Robin's eyes, but he kept hold of the woman's foot.

This criminal was clearly a skilled fighter. But so was Robin!

He twisted her foot to the side. The move flipped the woman onto the ground. The Boy Wonder crouched to tie up her hands when something heavy landed on his back.

THUD!

It was the man! He had grabbed Robin from behind and now squeezed tight. Robin staggered to his feet and tried to spin the man off his back. The brute would not budge.

So the boy backed up hard into the alley wall. The criminal slammed into the bricks.

WHAM!

Still the man hung on. Finally, Robin kicked up his feet and fell onto his back, throwing them both flat to the ground.

"*OOF!*" The man landed with a grunt. As he lay on the ground, catching his breath, Robin bounced onto his feet.

With the two goons dazed and defeated, Robin looked around for the third, most dangerous foe.

"No!" Robin shouted when he spotted the Super-Villain.

Catwoman was clutching the one thing he was supposed to keep safe—the package of alarm parts!

She had already managed to pick the lock on the case. She was practically purring over the sparkly contents inside.

"What's all this? Are you a rock collector now?" Catwoman asked. She slung the case's strap onto her shoulder and pulled out a crystal to admire its shine. "Or a jewel thief?"

"Get your paws off that!" Robin shouted.

"Or what?" Catwoman tossed the crystal into the air and caught it. "What would you do, little bird?"

Robin knew she was playing with him like a cat teasing a mouse. But with each toss of the crystal, his heart rose up to his throat and dropped back down to his chest.

"Be careful!" Robin said.

Catwoman tossed the crystal higher. "Why are you so worried about a few tiny rocks?" she asked with a sharp smile. "Are they important? Maybe you're planning to feather your nest with them?"

Robin lunged, trying to grab the container and the airborne crystal. Catwoman easily stepped out of the way. She wrapped her fist around the gem.

"And where are you taking them in the big city at dark?" the villain went on. "Don't you know it's dangerous out here all alone?"

Robin clenched his jaw. He had to get the crystals back!

"Get your paws off of Batman's crystals!" he shouted. He dove again.

Catwoman stuck out a booted leg, tripping Robin. He stumbled forward and felt his face grow hot.

Before he realized he had opened his mouth, Robin blurted out the last thing he meant to say: "Batman needs those at the museum!"

"Oh he does, does he?" Catwoman asked. Her eyebrows shot up sky-high. "And at the *museum*, you say? Aren't they going to be up to their necks in gems soon?"

A horrible feeling twisted Robin's stomach into a knot. He should not have said anything to the feline foe.

"*Hmmm*," Catwoman purred.

Her free hand drifted to her throat, as if to stroke an imaginary diamond necklace. She looked lost in a daydream while still tossing the crystal.

Robin saw his chance! He grabbed a trash can from the alley. Then he hurled it at Catwoman just as the crystal left her hand.

BANG!

The trash can slammed into the wall. Catwoman had leaped high, narrowly avoiding being hit.

In that split second, Robin sprang forward. He caught the crystal in midair.

"Gotcha!" he cried.

But he still needed the other crystals. Robin turned and saw the case on the ground. The precious package had slipped off Catwoman's shoulder!

The Boy Wonder scrambled for the case. His hand was just about to close around the strap when—

WHAM!

Robin crashed to the ground. The goon from the window was back in action and had rammed into him!

Robin staggered to his feet, looking all around. The man was right in front of him. The woman was standing once more and stalking forward. Catwoman had nabbed the case and held it tucked under one arm. With her other hand, she flicked her whip.

CRACK!

Robin needed a new plan. Even with all his training, he wasn't sure he could take on three criminals at once. The odds were not in his favor. He needed to get the case and go!

Tucking himself into a ball, Robin somersaulted past the big brute. Then in one motion, the acrobatic hero unfurled, sprang to his feet, and reached out a hand to grab his container.

Catwoman had no time to react.

"*NYYOOOOW!*" she yowled as he pulled the case away.

Robin did not stop to enjoy his victory. He quickly placed the crystal back inside the case as he picked up speed. His feet fell faster and faster. He blasted away from Catwoman and her cronies.

Robin ran without pausing to look back, even when he noticed that the only footsteps he could hear were his own. *Why aren't they coming after me?* he wondered.

As he ran out of the alley, the young Super Hero heard Catwoman's evil, purring laugh. Then her voice echoed off the brick buildings, saying, "Let the little bird go. We have bigger fish to fry!"

CHAPTER 4

HIDING IN PLAIN SIGHT

"Go straight to the museum. Do not stop along the way. Do not let that case out of your sight. And do not talk to strangers!"

Alfred's words echoed in Robin's head as he pulled up his hood to hide his identity once more. He returned to the red-dotted path charted out on his wrist screen and hurried toward his destination.

Why didn't I follow Alfred's advice? he thought as he moved through the streets.

The young hero knew why. He had wanted to stop a burglary. But instead, he had broken his promise and almost lost the parts he was supposed to deliver! Worst of all, he had revealed Batman's location to a dangerous foe.

Taking a deep breath, Robin patted the case of crystals. *At least the parts are safe and sound,* he thought. *The sooner I get them to Batman, the sooner the real treasure will be safe too. I just need to focus on my mission.*

Robin looked out at the setting sun. He could still deliver the crystals before nightfall, if he hurried.

The sun cast long shadows on the streets between the tall buildings downtown. Robin scuttled in the darkest of them, trying not to be noticed. He kept his feet moving and his head down.

Then at last, Robin saw the giant Gotham City Art Museum looming before him.

The front of the building was as fancy as a frosted cake. Signs at the top of the steps announced the museum was closed. Other signs with a photo of the impressive Dewdrop Diamond advertised the House of Jelenia's jewelry exhibit. They read *COMING SOON*.

Robin looked around to make sure nobody was watching. When the street was clear, he hurried into an alley.

The building was much plainer around back. The Boy Wonder came to a rear entrance.

He tried the door.

CLICK!

To his surprise, it opened. The door was unlocked.

The hairs on the back of Robin's neck stood up. It wasn't like the Dark Knight to leave a door unlocked and valuables unprotected. Carefully, he slipped inside.

Robin took cautious steps. They echoed on the marble floor.

TAP TAP TAP

The young hero expected to see Batman working away on the alarm system. All he found was a dark, empty room.

A dim light burned at the end of a shadowy walkway. Robin moved toward it. He knew Batman preferred the cover of night for most of his adventures. But it seemed strange to Robin that he was working on a complicated alarm system with most of the lights off.

"Batman?" Robin called out.

There was no answer.

He crept closer. A movement on the other side of the distant doorway caught his eye. A familiar shadow soon appeared. It was the dark silhouette of a head with two pointed ears.

"Batman?" Robin called again.

At last a voice answered in a low, raspy whisper. "Robin, is that you?"

"Yes, I've come to help. I've brought . . ." Robin trailed off.

Although the silhouette was familiar, Robin's gut twisted. It was telling him that something was not right. He stopped moving down the hallway.

But then the voice in his head argued, *You trusted your gut last time and look where it got you. You almost lost the crystals!*

Robin took a deep breath. He started inching closer.

"Batman, it's so dark in here," he said.

"The better to avoid detection, Boy Wonder," came the whispered response.

Robin took a few more steps toward the shadow. "Batman, why are you whispering? Why does your voice sound so strange?"

"The better to avoid being overheard, my young friend," was the hoarse reply.

After taking two more steps, the boy felt something bumpy beneath his feet.

Robin saw the silhouette move. On the ground, a shadow of clawed hands started reaching out.

"Batman, what sharp claws you have!" Robin exclaimed.

"The better to steal your treasure, little bird!" came the purred reply.

"Catwoman!" Robin yelled, just as Alfred's package was yanked from his grasp and the ground shifted beneath him.

FWIIIP!

A trap had been sprung! Robin was swallowed up into a net hanging from the ceiling.

Beneath him, Catwoman cackled greedily, clutching the container of crystals.

CHAPTER 5

THE END

Robin struggled to break out of the net holding him over the marble floor.

"What have you done with Batman?" he yelled.

Catwoman gave the net a small push. "Why? Are you hoping he'll save you? Hoping he'll come to let his little bird out of this cage?" she asked, watching Robin sway back and forth. She chuckled. "I'm afraid your big, bad bat is tied up right now."

Catwoman strode over to a row of light switches on the wall. She flipped them all at once, and everything came into clear focus.

Around the large display room, broken glass sparkled on the floor. All the cases had been smashed and now stood empty. Catwoman had bagged the gems!

Still swinging in his rope prison, Robin strained his neck. He tried to take in the whole terrible scene.

"Looking for this?" Catwoman asked.

The burglar pulled a huge green gem from a velvet bag she was holding beside Alfred's container. The Dewdrop Diamond glinted in the light.

"Or that?" She nodded to the side.

Robin gasped as he saw a sight more horrible than Catwoman's haul.

The real Batman was being held by Catwoman's two cronies!

The Super Hero's hands and feet were tied tightly together. A gag covered his mouth. The pair of goons from earlier stood on either side of him, gripping his arms.

Batman struggled to pull free. He tried to call out to his young crime-fighting partner through the gag. But Robin couldn't make out a word.

Robin shuddered and squeezed his fists on the ropes of the net. Catwoman had gotten to the unprotected treasure *and* Batman. Even worse, it was all his fault!

He had failed in his solo mission. But he was going to make things right.

"You're never going to get away with this!" Robin shouted.

"Ha!" Catwoman laughed as she slid the Dewdrop into the case with the crystal parts. Then she dropped in the velvet bag holding the rest of the stolen jewels.

"And how exactly does the caged bird think he's going to stop me?" she asked. "By squawking?"

The thief was so busy gloating, she didn't see the Boy Wonder moving in his rope prison. She didn't see that he had been reaching for something on his Utility Belt.

Robin quickly took out a sharp Batarang. He worked with small movements. He cut through one, two, three strands of the net. Until . . .

THUD!

The trap unraveled! Robin landed hard onto the ground.

Catwoman hissed. "Naughty bird!"

She dropped the case of loot beside her feet and readied her whip. She snapped it at the young hero.

CRACK!

Robin dodged to the side. The lash split the air right next to his head, making his ears ring. But he did not stop.

He dove for the container and knocked it away from Catwoman. The case tipped onto its side as it slid across the floor. The Dewdrop skittered out.

"Get my gems!" Catwoman yelled at her goons.

The man and woman let go of Batman and started to scramble for the precious jewels.

As soon as the pair released his arms, Batman sprang into action. He swung his bound fists fast and hard to his left.

WHOMP!

The henchman let out a grunt as the air was knocked out of him. He crashed to the floor.

Meanwhile, Robin grabbed a small stepladder Batman had been using to install the alarm system. He hurled it toward the running woman.

"*ARGH!*" the goon cried as the ladder sent her sprawling.

Robin leaped over his fallen foe to make a grab for the loose diamond. But he was too late. Catwoman dashed in and came up with the Dewdrop first.

The crook held the sparkling gem in her black-gloved hand and flashed a smile.

Robin saw her eyes dart toward the door. She had a clean shot at escape!

With Batman busy loosening his bindings, the Boy Wonder needed to act fast.

FWOOOOP!

He whipped off the special cape Alfred had given him and hurled it at Catwoman.

The surprised crook yowled as the heavy fabric tangled around her head, neck, and shoulders. Robin leaped onto Catwoman's back and held the hood over her face.

Catwoman let out a muffled growl and staggered around blindly. She still held the giant gem in one hand and her whip in the other. She would need to let go of one of them to get Robin and his fighting hood off of her!

SNAP!

Catwoman spun around and flicked her lash in anger, like an impatient cat twitching its tail.

SNAP!

She flicked the whip again, but this time Batman caught the snapping leather with superfast reflexes. He had gotten free of his bindings!

The Dark Knight jerked the whip, pulling Catwoman off balance. Robin leaped off her back as Batman quickly wrapped the long strap around her again and again. It held her arms tight against her sides.

MROWWRR!

With a yowl, Catwoman toppled to the ground. She twisted and wriggled, but she couldn't get free.

Robin easily took the Dewdrop Diamond from the thief's hand. He stood by his mentor's side.

"Well, that wraps things up!" the boy said.

"Just about," Batman replied. He tossed a pair of Bat-Cuffs he kept on his Utility Belt over to his young partner.

Robin caught them and worked on securing Catwoman's dazed cronies while Batman called the Gotham City police. When Robin had finished, he picked up the fallen case from the floor.

"Is this everything?" Robin asked Batman, handing him the Dewdrop Diamond and the case that Alfred had packed.

Batman peered inside the container. He unloaded the velvet bag of jewels and the crystals. Then he reached in farther.

"Yes, and a little something extra!" Batman said. He smiled beneath his cowl. "Our butler friend always seems to be one step ahead of us."

Batman pulled out a small package that had been tucked in the bottom of the container. Inside was a snack for two.

Robin smiled too, as his stomach growled. *Alfred thinks of everything! How does he know I'm hungry even before I do?* he wondered.

"Come, Robin. Let's eat," Batman said. "It's important to keep our energy up and be ready for anything!"

While Batman laid out the food, Robin took his cape from Catwoman's head.

I'm glad the mission was a success in the end, the boy thought, *but I should've listened to Alfred from the start!*

He would certainly never take the butler's wise words for granted again.

Robin folded the cape into a square. It had come in handy in more ways than one today. The hiding hood had become his fighting hood. And there was still one last purpose it could serve.

Placing the folded fabric on the floor, Robin took a seat on his makeshift cushion across from Batman. Then the Dynamic Duo dug in.

THE ORIGINAL STORY:
Little Red Riding Hood

Once upon a time, there lived a girl who everyone called Little Red Riding Hood. One day, Red's mother asked her to take a basket of cakes to her sickly grandmother, saying, "Do not stray from the path. Do not talk to strangers."

Red set off into the woods and soon met a wolf. Forgetting her mother's warning, she told him about her trip. The wolf asked where the grandmother lived and suggested the girl pick flowers to bring with the cakes. Then he rushed away.

Red gathered flowers and continued to her grandmother's. The door was already open. Inside, Red could see a nightcap peeking above the quilts on the bed. But something was odd. The girl noted the old woman's big ears and eyes. The person under the quilts explained them away. Finally Red said, "Grandmother, what big teeth you have!"

"The better to eat you with, my dear!" came the reply. Then the wolf, dressed in the grandmother's nightgown, jumped out of bed and swallowed Red Riding Hood whole!

Not long after, a hunter heard snores coming from the house. He found the big-bellied wolf sleeping soundly. He opened the beast's mouth, and out sprang Red and her grandmother, alive! The wolf awoke, but the sight of the hunter scared him to death. Then the girl, the old woman, and the hunter enjoyed every bit of cake in the basket. And Little Red Riding Hood vowed never to talk to strangers or stray from the forest path again.

SUPERPOWERED TWISTS

- Red Riding Hood walks into the woods to bring a basket of cakes to her sick grandmother. Robin secretly moves through Gotham City on a mission to deliver alarm parts to Batman.

- Both kids in the tales have trouble following directions, and it leads to big trouble. Red forgets her mother's warning when she talks to the wolf. Robin ignores Alfred's advice and stops to break up a burglary.

- The girl in the fairy tale is known for her red cape. Robin usually wears a yellow cape, but Alfred adds a hood to help hide the boy's identity.

- The wolf and Catwoman stop the young heroes on their way. But both villains let them go and then race off to their destinations in search of larger rewards.

- Red gets gobbled up by the wolf. Robin gets snapped up by the cat burglar's net.

- In the fairy tale, a hunter saves the girl and her grandmother from the wolf. In this adventure, Robin and Batman work together to defeat Catwoman!

TALK ABOUT IT

1. Describe how Robin feels about his mission when Alfred first explains it. How does Robin's attitude change throughout the story? Use examples to support your answer.

2. When Robin enters the museum, what clues are there that it's really Catwoman waiting for him, not Batman? Try to find at least three.

3. Robin wishes that he had listened to Alfred's advice. Have you ever regretted not listening to someone? If you could go back in time, would you do things differently?

WRITE ABOUT IT

1. Did Robin make the right decision when he stopped to try to tie up the thieves? Write a paragraph arguing for your answer.

2. How do you think Catwoman and her goons managed to capture Batman? You can either write the story from the Super Hero's point of view or the Super-Villain's!

3. Fairy tales are often told and retold over many generations, and the details can change depending on who tells them. Write your version of the "Little Red Riding Hood" story. Change a lot or a little, but make it your own!

The Author

Sarah Hines Stephens lives a fairy tale life in Oakland, California, with her two magical kids, a pair of charming dogs, and a prince of a husband. If she could pick a superpower, it would definitely be flight so she could zoom all over the world having adventures, trying out new foods, and visiting far-flung friends and family. Sarah has written over one hundred books for kids about all kinds of crazy characters—none of whom hold a candle to the wacky cast she loves and lives with.

The Illustrators

Agnes Garbowska is an artist who has worked with many major book publishers, illustrating such brands as DC Super Hero Girls, Teen Titans Go!, My Little Pony, and Care Bears. She was born in Poland and came to Canada at a young age. Being an only child, she escaped into a world of books, cartoons, and comics. She currently lives in the United States and enjoys sharing her office with her two little dogs.

Sil Brys is a colorist and graphic designer. She has worked on many comics and children's books, having had fun coloring stories for Teen Titans Go!, Scooby-Doo, Tom & Jerry, Looney Tunes, DC Super Hero Girls, Care Bears, and more. She lives in a small village in Argentina, where her home is also her office. She loves to create there, surrounded by forests, mountains, and a lot of books.